Fake Identity
True Love

Friends to Lovers Sweet Romance Short Stories Collection

Eva Stone

Contents

The Mysterious Homeless Man

I am going to the library on Saturday afternoon to do more research for my graduate school assignment. As I pass by a fast-food restaurant, the rain suddenly becomes heavy. Raindrops as big as grapes fall heavily on the red brick walkway. I seek refuge from the relentless rain when I run to the restaurant. I find a homeless man standing on the corner near the entry door.

Everyone rushes by, oblivious to the lone figure huddled against the elements. His presence tugs at my heart, a vivid contrast to the bustling indifference around us.

"Hello there," I say, turning to him. "Would you like a meal?"

Despite his unkempt appearance, the man before me meets my gaze, and I see intelligence sparkling in his eyes. He is tall, and his spirit radiates with humor and wit. "Well, I'd be a fool to turn down an offer like that." He chuckles, his voice carrying warmth and mischief.

"Come in, please."

"No. No one wants to see me inside. I can wait here."

I run into the fast-food restaurant, and the aromas of greasy fries and sizzling burgers fill the air. I stand in the line and realize I forgot to ask the homeless man what he wants. So, I walk out and head to him.

"Sir, what do you want?"

The water falling from the roofline forms a water screen between us. My jeans are wet up to my calf.

This time, this man does not smile. He looks at my eyes and says, "Anything you give me."

"I want to give you something you like. Chicken or beef?"

"Anything you like."

I return to the restaurant. By the time I walk out, I bring two warm burgers; one is a chicken burger, and another one is a beef burger. I bid him farewell and go to the library, immersing myself in books and knowledge. Hours pass in the quiet solitude of the library. The storm outside cannot bother me.

When I finally decide to head home, the night has draped itself in darkness. As I enter the rain-soaked streets, I am surprised to find the homeless man sitting outside the fast-food restaurant. It will be cold tonight, and he must be soaked from the earlier storms.

I approach him once more. "You're still here," I start to worry for him.

He nods, his eyes mirroring the rain-soaked pavement. "It's where I stay," he replies with a hint of resignation.

Without hesitation, I make a heartfelt offer. "Would you like to come with me? I have a place where you can stay for the night, and I can prepare a simple dinner."

His face lights up, and his gratitude shines through. "That's very kind of you," he says, his voice brimming with sincerity. "I'd be honored to accept your offer. But I do not want to bother your family."

"I live alone. My roommate has her private bedroom." He is a thoughtful man.

Together, we leave the stormy streets behind and find our way to my modest abode, where warmth and companionship replace the cold and loneliness of the outside world.

"Sit down, please." I share a living room and kitchen with my roommate. I point at the creamy couch—it's mine.

He glances at the spotless couch, then comes to my tiny dining table near the kitchen and sits on the dining chair. He does not want to get my couch dirty.

I cook a simple dinner. We have a few moments of eye contact. I have never brought any stranger into my room, but I'm doing the right thing to help this man.

I bring salad and sandwiches to the table.

"May I?" He looks at his hands and asks.

"Follow me, please." I lead him to my bathroom. He washes his hands twice and does not miss his fingernails.

We have dinner quietly. Under the soft glow of the dining light, I notice he is a good-looking guy, and his fingernails look neater than mine.

I say gently. "I'm Nancy. May I know your name?"

With a quick wit and a hint of humor in his eyes, the homeless man replies, "You can call me PG."

"PG?"

"Short for 'poor guy'."

We share a moment of laughter as the rain continues to pour. At this point, Cindy, my roommate, returns from work.

"Good rain," she says as she walks in. She has a car, and she is still dry.

"Sorry, I did not know you had a guest." She peers her head from the entry of the living room, then back to her room. Curly red hair almost obscures half her face, but I can still see her making a face to me as she notices PG.

I started cleaning the kitchen and washing the dishes. PG sits on the chair calmly.

I hope he can stand up and say goodbye to me, but he has not and possibly will not. It's still raining. What should I do next? Should I ask him to leave? I may bring trouble to myself.

Despite our little connection during our meal, I feel uncomfortable letting him stay in the living room. My roommate may not like that idea. But she will not mind if I let PG sleep in my room.

So, I make a generous offer. "PG, would you like to stay here tonight? I can spend the night with my roommate."

GP nods. Gratitude washes over his face as he accepts my offer. I put a new bath towel in the bathroom and pick up my blue sleeping bag from the closet.

"Good night, PG."

"Good night, Nancy."

A few seconds later, I'm inside Cindy's room. We have been roommates for two years. We are as close as sisters.

"Is he your relative?" Cindy looks down from her bed. There are hundreds of question marks on her face. She is usually not that curious.

"No. I met him on the street." I slip into my sleeping bag and feel the floor is so hard.

"You are damn brave; you could have invited danger to our home." Cindy jumps down and locks the bedroom door angrily.

I do not blame her. The night passes slowly, with my thoughts often drifting back to the stranger named PG. I'm curious if he's comfortable in my bedroom. Is he warm and dry now? I hope he's okay.

The following morning, I knocked on my door with trepidation and curiosity. No response.

As I step inside, I'm met with a sight that utterly astonishes me. My typically messy home has been transformed into a place of pristine cleanliness. It's as though a fairy with a penchant for tidiness has visited overnight.

PG did not touch my bed.

I marvel at the orderliness of my surroundings, my heart swelling with gratitude and disbelief. On my glass end table, I discover a beautifully crafted thank-you note. It's a work of art, a testament to PG's thoughtfulness and appreciation for my kindness.

The note reads:

Dear Nancy, Thank you for your generosity and compassion. Your kindness has touched my heart, and I wanted to express my gratitude in the best way I know how. Sincerely, PG.

Tears well up in my eyes as I read those heartfelt words. In offering PG shelter for the night, I realize I received a gift far more significant than I expected—a reminder that despite life's storms, there is room for unexpected connections, kindness, and the beauty of human compassion.

PG may have called himself a "poor guy," but in my eyes, he was the wealthiest soul I had ever met. This extraordinary encounter served as a testament to the power of kindness and the beauty of shared humanity.

The next few days, I always look for PG when I pass by the restaurant. But I will never see him again. He seems to have disappeared from the city, from my life too.

Weeks later, I'm walking down the same busy street, and there he is again, PG, sitting outside the fast-food joint. The streetlights' soft glow dimly lights the road, and the previous week's rain has given way to a chilly breeze. The restaurant's bright neon sign flickers, casting a warm light on the damp pavement.

I decide to seize the moment and approach PG. "Hey again, PG!" I'm so happy to find him again.

He looks up, his eyes crinkling at the corners as he smiles back. "Hey," he replies, his voice carrying a quiet warmth that contrasts with the chill in the air.

We sit down together on the sidewalk, and I notice a few disapproving glances from people passing by. Their expressions aren't cheerful, but I ignore them and focus on the conversation with PG.

"How about dinner tonight? My treat."

PG hesitates for a moment, then nods appreciatively. "That sounds good. Thanks."

We chat about various topics—books, movies, favorite local spots—all in a short but friendly exchange. PG's replies may be concise but laced with intelligence and depth.

I ask him, "What's your favorite book?"

He leans in as if sharing a secret and says, "*One Hundred Years of Solitude* by Gabriel García Márquez. It's like a journey through time and memory."

His response catches me off guard, and I smile, genuinely impressed. "I love that one too," I admit. "Magical realism at its finest."

PG nods, his eyes lighting up. "Exactly! It's like stepping into a dream."

As the night deepens, our conversation flows easily, and I am more drawn to PG. Despite his few words, something is captivating about the way he speaks. He's a fantastic person, and his quiet respectfulness adds to his appeal.

I've seen PG as extraordinary proof that sometimes the most exciting people are the ones you least expect to meet.

Months have passed, and winter has firmly gripped the city. The days are growing colder, and I follow my usual routine, often walking by that familiar fast-food restaurant. But I last saw PG a long time ago. I start worrying about him.

It's a snowy evening, and the world is draped in a soft, white veil. The street is calm, with the only sounds being the muffled footsteps of passersby and the occasional car gliding by. The frosted windows of the restaurant cast a warm and inviting glow onto the chilly pavement outside.

Approaching my apartment building, I spot PG huddled in a corner, his body trembling from the cold. Concern propels me forward, and I hurry over to him.

"PG, it's freezing out here," I exclaim, the frosty air stinging my cheeks.

He looks up, a weary but grateful smile on his face. "You're telling me," He replies with a hint of humor, his breath forming tiny clouds in the frigid air.

"PG, it's getting late and so cold outside. Why don't you stay in my apartment tonight?"

PG looks at me, hesitating.

"Come with me, please." I want to bring PG to my apartment.

"No, but thank you."

"How about having a hot meal?" I keep trying.

"I do not want to bother you again," PG is hard-headed.

"I thought we were friends. But you are so distant, PG."

PG's eyes reflect gratitude but also determination. "Nancy, I appreciate it, but I can't impose on you like that. I'll find a place to stay."

I respect his choice but want to ensure he's safe and warm. So, I gather all the cash I have, about $55, and hand it to him. "Please, take this. Get yourself a warm jacket and find shelter for the night."

PG accepts the money, his eyes conveying appreciation. "Thank you, Nancy," he says, his voice sincere. "You've been incredibly kind."

I watch him disappear into the snowy night. The mixture of emotions inside me deepens. At this moment, amidst the falling snowflakes. PG is homeless, but he is a very respectful person.

After the new year, my article is published in a famous magazine. And then, I surprisingly receive an invitation to attend a publishing conference. I'm so excited about it.

The event is in a grand convention center with authors, publishers, and literary enthusiasts. The lobby buzzes with excitement as participants exchange ideas and discuss their latest projects.

As I browse the conference agenda, I focus on a keynote speaker who resembles PG. The speaker's name is Paul Gibson. The mere thought sends a shiver down my spine and my heart races. It can't be him, can it?

When the time comes for this mysterious speaker to take the stage, I find myself on edge, my nerves tingling with anticipation. As he begins to speak, my suspicions intensify. It's PG's voice, unmistakable and hauntingly familiar.

Does PG have a twin brother? Until this moment, I realize I know nothing about PG.

During the lunch break, I go to the dining hall, a bustling room filled with round tables and animated conversations. I stand there, lost in a sea of faces, unsure what to do next. That's when I see him.

PG enters the hall with a group of well-dressed and important-looking people. He moves with a confident stride, his presence commanding the attention of those around him. My heart leaps into my throat, and I feel a rush of emotions—surprise, disbelief, an overwhelming desire to reconnect, and a little anger.

He approaches, our eyes locking, and he calls out my name. "Nancy!"

I stand there, stunned and speechless for a moment. Then, the anger and sense of betrayal surge forward, and I finally find my voice, though it trembles with emotion. "PG! Is that you? How could you...?" I can't speak anymore.

"Nancy, I'm so sorry. It just... happened."

My frustration simmers as I look at his eyes. What I want to say is: "Just happened? You left me hanging, wondering what happened to you. I thought you were homeless, struggling to survive!" But I bite my lip and don't let these words out in front of others.

PG looks at me with mixed emotion, his voice low and irresistible. "How about dinner tonight? My treat."

It was the words I spoke to him. He even copies my tone.

"That sounds good. Thanks."

We both repeated the exact words, but the roles have switched.

Then, he walks away with the others.

For the rest of the conference, I'm lost. I expect dinner to arrive.

The night has fallen, and the conference is finally over. I take my time dressing up for the dinner party, choosing an elegant outfit. I head to the dining hall and find my way to the table, where I wait for PG.

Moments later, he arrives, but he looks different. No name tag, no suit; instead, he's dressed in business casual attire. There's a sense of transformation about him, and I can't help but feel curious and slightly puzzled.

I beckon him to sit, and as we settle into our chairs, he explains, "Nancy, I have to tell you something. It's not easy."

I nod, my curiosity deepening as I encourage him to continue.

With a sigh, PG begins his story. "I'm not who I pretended to be," he admits, his gaze locked on mine. "I'm a billionaire. I was tired of being pursued for my wealth, and I wanted to find a genuine connection. I wanted to meet someone who cared about me for who I am, not for my money."

His confession surprises me, and I can hardly believe what I hear. "So, you're saying... all this time, you've been pretending to be homeless?"

PG smiles. "Not all the time. Most days, I still have to return to manage my business." A mixture of regret and hope is in his eyes. "Yes, Nancy. I disguised myself as a homeless man to find a true connection. And then, I met you."

I sit there, absorbing the weight of his words, grappling with the deception and the truth behind his actions. "But why didn't you tell me the truth earlier?" I ask, my voice filled with a sense of betrayal.

He reaches out, his hand gently covering mine. "I'm so sorry, Nancy. I didn't want to scare you away. I wanted to be sure you liked me for who I am. Even if I'm homeless, we can share something in common."

Emotions swirl within me, a mix of anger, disbelief, and an undeniable connection that has grown between us. "Do you... do you love me?" I finally ask, my voice shaking.

PG gazes at me with sincerity and vulnerability. "Yes, Nancy. I love you. I did plan for this, but my feelings for you are genuine."

"I'm not pretty. I'm just one of the most ordinary people."

"You are the one I've been searching for. You have a beautiful heart. I trust that you will never betray me, whether I'm rich or poor. You are the one I want to share my entire life with."

Tears well up in my eyes, and despite the web of lies, I realize that my feelings for him run deep. "I love you too, PG."

In that moment, our love transcends deception, and we embrace the connection that has grown between us, uncertain of the future but willing to face it together.

The soft, melodic strains of music fill the air as the evening transitions into party time. The room is aglow with warm, inviting light, and the atmosphere is electric with the promise of joy and celebration.

Amid the lively crowd, PG extends his hand toward me, his eyes locking on mine with a warm, inviting smile. "Nancy, would you care to dance with me?"

I take his hand without hesitation, and we move gracefully to the dance floor. PG's movements are effortless, and he leads with a confident grace that leaves me utterly enchanted. His charisma radiates, making him even more handsome and captivating in my eyes.

As we sway to the rhythm of the music, it feels as though the world outside this moment doesn't exist. Our laughter mingles with the melodies, and I can't help but be drawn further into PG's magnetic presence.

"PG, it is our happy night."

"Nancy, it is the beginning of our happy life."

Chasing Shadows of the Heart

I'm on a busy downtown street taking photos for a travel magazine. I've got my camera up, scanning for a good shot when I see her. She stands out from the crowd, catching my eye like something special.

I'm trying to get a great photo, and she's different. She looks right at me, strong and intense. Then, clear and firm, she says, "Stop. I do not want to be in your picture." Her voice is full of annoyance but also something like a challenge.

I put my camera down and meet her intense look. Her eyes are this amazing hazel, full of all these emotions. I can see she's mad, but it's not just that. She's interesting, more than just her anger.

This throws me off.

"Sorry," I say, giving her a guilty smile and showing I mean no harm. "I didn't mean to crash into your privacy like that."

She tells me to delete the picture immediately.

Walking over, I give her my business card with both hands, trying to smooth things over.

She gives me this half-smile that lets me know she's less mad now. "So, you're Alex, the photographer," she says, looking closer at me.

Her tone gives away a hint of hope, so I take a shot, "Can I keep the photo? It's the best one I took today."

But she's firm. "No. You can snap anything else around here. There's plenty to tell on this street, but I'm not one of those stories." Even as she speaks sharply, a twinkle in her eye suggests she's partly in jest.

I get the message; the photo has to go. "You know, moments like this are what it's all about," I tell her, keeping it light and nodding towards the busy scene around us. "Life in its pure form. Old buildings and new ones side by side, like the past and future mingled together."

She looks at me, her annoyance fading as fast as it appeared. "I guess you have a point," she admits, and I can see her relax a bit.

The air between us changes, becoming lighter and filled with a mutual curiosity. She's got stories hidden deep in those hazel eyes, and I'm drawn to them, wanting to peel back the layers of her initial resistance.

The city moves indifferently around us. Still, this little friction has sparked something, a connection neither of us expected.

"What's your name?" I ask.

She hesitates, then, with a slight pause, says, "You can call me Sophia."

It fits her perfectly.

"Sophia, how about you join me for dinner?" I ask, hoping to extend this unexpected encounter.

She sizes me up, weighing her options, then declines, "No."

"Not dinner then, just a drink for happy hour. I promise, no pressure."

Then, that enigmatic smile lights up her face, and she agrees with a nod. Leaning in, her eyes twinkle with a hint of trouble. "I'm in for dinner, but on one condition."

Curious, I lift an eyebrow. "Oh? And what's that?"

With a mischievous grin, she lays down her rule. "I pick the place."

I laugh, realizing she's got a mind of her own. "Deal. You call the shots tonight."

Sophia takes me to this cozy Thai place a couple of blocks away. Its welcoming, bright yellow doors and elephant statue greet us. The smell of spices hits me, promising a meal to remember.

Now, the challenge is deciding what to order. I know nothing about Thai food.

"How do you feel about spicy food, Alex? Their red curry is legendary."

She's got this look like she's plotting something fun. I hesitate, then blurt out, "Sure." The truth is, my relationship with spicy food is more miss than hit, but I'm not about to show weakness.

Her smile widens, "Trust me, you don't want to miss this. Let's get you that red curry."

Before I know it, she's ordered for me, and I'm bracing myself for impact. When the curry arrives, I'm mentally preparing for an adventure.

As I take the first bite, her eyes are glued to me, filled with anticipation. Instantly, I'm a mess. Sweat beads on my forehead, and my eyes water as if I'm cutting onions.

Sophia can barely contain her laughter. "You good?"

I'm fighting for composure, my voice strained. "Absolutely, just enjoying the ride."

Her laughter fills the restaurant, reminding me of simpler times. Despite the heat, this moment of shared joy over my culinary misstep brings us closer.

The Thai restaurant glows warmly around us, our laughter blending into the cozy atmosphere. Despite the initial challenge posed by the spicy dish, the evening unfolds into a beautiful adventure.

As we talk more, finding common ground in our love for the arts, it feels like we're moving closer, both physically and metaphorically. The night deepens, and we almost forget the world outside, lost in our conversation and the connection that seems to grow stronger by the minute.

But then, a commotion interrupts our bubble. We look at each other, puzzled, and then Sophia's face changes; she knows she needs to leave. "I'm sorry, Alex," she tells me regretfully. "I have to go."

I try to keep it light, masking my disappointment. "No worries. Sometimes, you gotta do what you gotta do."

After a brief goodbye, she's off, vanishing into the night as quickly as she came into my life. Left in the quiet after her departure, I can't help but feel a mix of sadness and hope. Our brief connection was unexpectedly deep; now, I'm left wishing for another chance to see her.

And then, as I sit there, it dawns on me—I never got her phone number.

Feeling regret and hope, I pay the bill and return to the night. The cool air hits me, reminding me that this evening with Sophia might be the beginning of something special. But in a city this big, finding her again feels like looking for a needle in a haystack.

I can't shake off the memory of our time together – her laugh, her eyes sparkled, and that undeniable connection. I'm determined to see her again, but all I have to go on is a handful of photos and the vivid impression she's left on me.

Back home, I pore over my camera's pictures, searching for any trace of her. I've already deleted that confrontational snapshot, but there's a chance she's somewhere in the others, caught accidentally in a frame.

As I sift through the images, time stretches out. I'm looking for that unique smile that's been etched into my mind. The endless parade of faces and places begins to blur, leaving me feeling lost.

But then, I see her. In the backdrop of a photo, there is a figure that makes my heart skip. Zooming in, I can hardly believe it – Sophia is walking out of a Cafe. I quickly save this precious clue.

With a burst of excitement, I know my next step. I have to return to that street, the place where everything started.

With Sophia's photo as my guide, I dive back into the downtown crowd, heart thumping with the hope of finding her again. She's sparked something in me I just can't shake off. I'm outside a quaint café, the ninth stop in my relentless search.

Crossing the threshold, the scent of coffee wraps around me, a comforting embrace. Conversation murmurs fill the space, lending it an intimate vibe. This café feels like a secret haven in the city's hustle, a spot ripe for confessions and tales waiting to be told.

Approaching the counter, I notice a red-haired lady with warm, welcoming eyes. From her name tag, I know her name is Elena. She's busy preparing drinks for the customers.

I take a deep breath and step forward, determined to find any information that could lead me to Sophia. "Excuse me, I'm looking for someone, and I heard she's been here before. Her name is Sophia." Then I show her Sophia's photo.

Elena pauses in her task and looks at the photo thoughtfully. "Sophia, you say? She's not a regular here, but I remember her pretty face. She came in a few times, always alone, and did not talk to anyone."

My heart skips a beat, and I lean in closer, eager for details. "Do you know anything about Sophia? Any way I could reach her?"

Elena nods, her eyes holding a hint of curiosity. "She was a bit of a mystery. She was always lost in thought as if she carried the world's weight. She had an artistic air, like a painter searching for inspiration."

I feel a pang of longing. "Is there anything else you remember that could help me find her?"

Elena smiles, a knowing twinkle in her eye. "Well, bookstore, maybe? She carried a bag of new books once. There is a bookshop just around the corner. Maybe you'll have better luck finding her there."

Gratitude wells up inside me as I thank Elena for her information. With renewed hope, I exit the café, the scent of coffee lingering in the air as I head toward the bookshop, my next destination in this pursuit of the enigmatic Sophia.

With Elena's cryptic hint about the bookshop, I find myself standing in front of the quaint little store around the corner. As I step inside, the smell of books and the soft creaking of wooden floors greet me.

As I browse the shelves, my mind races with thoughts of Sophia. I wonder what secrets lie hidden beneath her enigmatic exterior. Elena's description of Sophia as an artist searching for inspiration keeps playing in my mind.

Just as I'm about to leave, I overhear a conversation at the counter. An elderly customer is raving about the live music performances at a nearby concert hall, mentioning a talented musician named Sophia.

My heart skips a beat as I connect the dots.

Sophia—a musician?

I approach the elderly customer who mentioned Sophia, and my curiosity is piqued.

"Excuse me, I overheard you talking about a musician named Sophia. Can you tell me more about her?"

The elderly customer smiles with joy, "Of course! Sophia is an incredible musician. She's in her late twenties, with long, flowing dark hair and a captivating stage presence."

I eagerly ask, "Do you know when and where her next performance is?"

The elderly customer checks his phone slowly and then looks at me. "Her next show is tomorrow night at seven at the Hilton Concert Hall. It's an experience you won't want to miss!"

I sigh gratefully. "Thank you so much for the information! I appreciate it."

As I gather the details, excitement bubbles within me. Sophia, I will find you tomorrow.

The following day, before 7:00 p.m., the Hilton Concert Hall in the heart of downtown comes alive with anticipation.

I'm standing at the big front door, feeling super excited, and my heart is beating fast. I'm here because of how strongly I feel about Sophia and buzzing with energy.

As the doors open, I hear the buzz of people talking and see the gentle light filling up the room. So many people are around, all looking forward to hearing Sophia's music.

The crowd falls into a hushed reverence as the lights dim and the stage comes alive. And then, Sophia appears—a vision in the spotlight, the enigmatic musician I've been searching for, now stands before us.

Holding her guitar, Sophia starts to play, and her voice, captivating as ever, fills the room. Her music is more than just sounds; it's a peek into who she is. She sings about love, yearning, and what it means to be human.

I'm totally drawn in by the beauty of her tunes and the honest feelings in her singing. Every song feels like she's sharing a secret with me, letting me see a part of her heart. It's like she's singing just for me.

When she finishes her last song, everyone claps loudly. Sophia's smile is bright and genuine as she says thanks and steps back from the mic.

I can't wait any more. My heart pushes me through the crowd until I stand right before her. She looks surprised to see me there.

"Sophia," my voice filled with awe and admiration, "your music is incredible."

She turns to me, her gaze holding a mix of curiosity and vulnerability. "You found me."

I smile, my determination paying off. "I had to. After all, you're the missing piece of the puzzle."

Sophia's gaze softens, and she leans closer as if drawn by an invisible force. "What do you want, Alex?"

I take a step closer, my heart laid bare. "I want to know you, Sophia. The real you, the artist, the musician, the woman behind the mystery."

She stares at me, her gaze piercing into my eyes as if trying to glimpse into my heart. "This goes beyond my expectations, but I do want to get to know you better, too," she says softly, a hint of vulnerability in her words.

In the following weeks, I met with Sophia a few times. I notice that she's avoiding any conversation about her personal life. Questions about her background or dreams are met with a gentle but evasive smile, deepening the mystery surrounding her.

I start feeling frustrated because I want to know more about her and understand her. I try to get her to share more with me, but she's not ready to open up. This starts causing problems between us, turning our smooth connection into one with bumps and misunderstandings.

One evening, after yet another elusive response from her about her personal life, I can't hold back my frustration any longer. "Sophia, why are you keeping so much hidden? Is it so wrong for me to want to know you better?"

She sighs, her eyes filling with a mix of sorrow and determination. "Alex, you have to understand... I'm not like other people. I have my reasons for being guarded."

The tension between us rises as our differences come to the forefront. I, an open book, wear my heart on my sleeve while Sophia, the enigmatic musician, guards her emotions fiercely.

"The more I care about you," I confess, my voice tinged with desperation, "the more you become a mystery to me. I just want to be a part of your world."

Sophia looks away, her expression conflicted. "Alex, you have no idea what you're asking for."

The fight leaves a heavy silence between us as if we're being pushed apart by the things we can't agree on. We're both stubborn and full of love, but our own worries and doubts are getting in the way.

The days after our fight are tense. It seems like we're both trying to avoid making it worse, but it just makes everything feel more awkward.

I can't stand feeling so far from her anymore, so one night, I decide it's time to talk and try to overcome the barriers she's put up around her.

"Sophia," I say gently, "we can't go on like this. You've become a mystery I can't unravel, tearing us apart."

She sighs, and I can see sadness and resignation in her eyes. "I didn't want to burden you with my past, Alex. It's a painful part of my life I've tried to leave behind."

My heart aches at the vulnerability in her voice. "You don't have to carry it alone, Sophia. We can face it together."

She takes a deep breath, her fingers trembling slightly. "Okay, Alex. It's time you knew the truth." Sophia's voice quivers as she reveals the painful story she's kept hidden for so long. "It all happened on a night I'll never forget. I was at a party, and I lost track of time. My parents were on their way to pick me up. They never made it."

As Sophia opens up, her voice trembles with guilt and sorrow. She recounts the tragic accident that claimed her parents' lives, her eyes glistening with unshed tears. "I was too caught up in my happiness that night and didn't go home when I should have. If I had been more responsible, they might still be alive."

I gently squeeze her hand, offering my support and understanding as she shares her painful past. "Sophia, it's not your fault," I say softly. "You were just a young girl, and accidents happen. Your parents wouldn't want you to carry this burden forever."

She looks at me, her eyes searching for solace. "I know, but it's haunted me for so long. I've never forgiven myself for what happened."

I pull her into a comforting embrace, holding her close. "You don't have to carry this guilt alone, Sophia. We'll face it together, and I'll be here for you every step of the way."

She looks into my eyes, and suddenly, the walls between us disappear. I realize that something important has changed in our relationship. But I need to recognize that Sophia still has another secret, one that is dangerous and uncertain. This secret will challenge our love and trust, leading us on a path with many surprises and unexpected turns.

Sophia and I continue to grow closer as the days turn into weeks.

One evening, under a sky filled with stars, we sit on a park bench, the world around us fading into the background. The cool breeze rustles the leaves, and the gentle sounds of the night seem to envelop us.

"I've always dreamt of traveling the world," I confess, my gaze fixed on the stars above. "Capturing the beauty of different cultures through my lens."

Sophia smiles, her eyes reflecting the moonlight. "That sounds incredible, Alex. And I'd love to be a part of your adventures."

Her words warm my heart, and I turn to her, my hand finding hers. "And what about you, Sophia? What are your dreams?"

She hesitates for a moment as if contemplating her answer. "I dream of sharing my music with the world," she finally says, her voice soft but determined. "I want to touch people's hearts and make them feel something."

I'm captivated by her passion and sincerity. "You already do that every time you play."

Our eyes meet, and at that moment, I realize that something profound has shifted between us. It's not just a connection anymore; it's deep and unconditional love.

Our bond deepens as the weeks become months, and we fall in love. Our personalities, once so different, complement each other perfectly. My openness balances her guardedness, and her sensitivity grounds my adventurous spirit.

We revel in the beauty of our shared moments—the sunsets we watch together, the late-night conversations that stretch into dawn, and how our hearts beat in harmony when we're close.

One evening, as we sit on the rooftop of a quiet café, I take her hand and look into her eyes. "Sophia," I say, my voice trembling with emotion, "Did I ever tell you I love you?"

Tears glisten in her eyes as she smiles, a smile that lights up my world. "I love you too, Alex."

While Sophia and I enjoy our growing love, a scary threat creeps into our lives. It's like a dark storm cloud on the horizon, disturbing our newfound peace.

One night, as we take a moonlit stroll through a park, an eerie sensation crawls up my spine—a feeling of being watched, hunted even. I grasp Sophia's hand tightly, my heart pounding in my chest.

"Sophia," I whisper, my voice trembling, "do you sense it too? Something's not right."

"What happened?"

"I feel we are followed."

Sophia's eyes widen in alarm, mirroring my unease. "Alex, it's as though my past has caught up with us."

"Your past?" I inquire, my curiosity mixed with concern.

"I was a runaway bride," she admits, her voice laced with vulnerability.

My heart aches at the confession, and I can't help but wonder about the untold story behind those words. "What happened?"

Sophia bites her lip and shakes her head, leaving me in the dark about the details of her past. However, I can sense the weight of her unspoken words, and I know there are still layers of her history that she's not ready to reveal.

We become more afraid as days turn into anxious nights. We see shadows moving in the corners of our eyes, and faceless dangers seem to be hiding nearby. It feels like someone is relentlessly pursuing us.

Who's behind it?

Why are they so determined to catch us?

What will come our way?

I start searching for Sophia on the internet. One fateful night, my restless curiosity leads me to an old, obscure newspaper article buried deep within the internet archives. The headline sends shivers down my spine: "Bride's Mysterious Disappearance on Wedding Day."

The photograph accompanying the article reveals a hauntingly familiar face—the missing bride, none other than Sophia.

I confront her with my discovery, my voice heavy with concern. "Sophia, is this you?"

Tears brim in her eyes as she nods, a shudder of fear running through her. "Yes, Alex. It's me. I ran away to escape a life I never wanted, but he is still hunting me."

I pull her into a comforting embrace, determined to protect her from the looming threat. "Tell me, Sophia. What happened? Why is he still after you?"

She takes a deep breath, her voice trembling as she unravels the painful past. "I was very lonely after my parents passed away. I was so young when I fell in love with him, Alex. I didn't know who he really was until it was too late. He's a criminal, involved in things I can't even speak of."

I listen intently, my heart aching for her. "And the wedding?"

She looks down, her voice barely above a whisper. "I was supposed to marry him. But as I stood in that white dress, I realized I couldn't go through with it. I couldn't tie myself to a life of darkness."

The pieces of the enigmatic puzzle finally fall into place—her evasiveness, constant movement, and aversion to being photographed—all connected to a past she's been desperately trying to escape.

I hold her tighter, understanding the gravity of her decision. "You did what you had to do, Sophia. But we'll face this together. I won't let him hurt you." I prepare to confront the shadows that haunt Sophia's past.

We sit in the dimly lit sanctuary of our living room, faces bathed in the soft glow of candlelight, and she begins to speak.

"My ex," she says, her voice quivering with fear and determination, "was not just an ordinary man, Alex. He was deeply involved in a criminal world—a drug dealer."

Her words hang heavily in the air, and I feel a shiver run down my spine. I can see the pain etched into the lines of her face as she continues.

"Our relationship began as something beautiful, but as I got to know him better, I discovered the darkness that consumed him. He wanted me to be a part of his dangerous world and share his secrets and crimes. When I refused, it turned into a nightmare. He was violent."

As I listen to her story, the room seems to close in. I can't imagine the terror she must have endured, the constant fear of being hunted down by a ruthless criminal.

Sophia's eyes glisten with unshed tears as she meets my gaze. "I had to run away, Alex. It was the only way to escape his grasp, to protect myself and those I love."

Her confession fills me with a profound sense of compassion and love. I take her trembling hand, squeezing it gently in a silent promise of support.

"We'll face this together, Sophia," I say, my voice unwavering. "We'll ensure that he can never harm you again."

I understand our love will face a tough challenge with her past and the danger looming. But in this difficult time, our connection will become even stronger. It will be like a strong fortress of love and strength, ready to withstand any problems.

A few days after Sophia shared her secret with me, I walk her home after her performance. The night is cloaked in darkness, and we find ourselves cornered in a dimly lit alley, the walls closing in around us. Sophia clings to my arm, fear etched across her face, but her eyes have a glimmer of determination.

The man from her past steps into the flickering pool of light, a sinister smile on his lips. "Well, well, well, Sophia. Thought you could run forever?"

My voice is steady, unwavering. "You won't harm her," I say firmly, placing myself between Sophia and her menacing pursuer.

He chuckles, the sound dripping with malice. "And who's going to stop me, lover boy?"

But Sophia is no longer the terrified woman who once fled from him. She steps forward, her voice quivering but filled with resolve. "I won't let you control my life anymore. It's over."

The tension in the air is palpable as the confrontation escalates. He, Sophia's ex, unleashes a torrent of threats and accusations, each word a weapon aimed at her heart.

"You thought you could escape me, Sophia?" he sneers, his voice dripping with venom. "You thought you could run away and start a new life?"

Sophia's eyes blaze with defiance as she stands her ground. "Yes, I did. And I won't let you destroy that life."

He scoffs, his anger intensifying. "You don't understand what you've gotten yourself into, Sophia. You don't know the depths of my reach."

I watch, my anger simmering, as he taunts her.

But Sophia remains resolute, her voice unwavering. "I may not know everything, but I won't let you control me anymore."

Their conversation is a battleground filled with emotional landmines and painful memories. Despite the danger, Sophia refuses to back down, and it becomes clear that this confrontation is a turning point in her battle to break free from her past.

I intervene, my words laced with conviction. "Sophia's made her choice, and it's not with you. It's with me."

The man's face contorts with rage, his eyes narrowing into a furious glare. "You think you can take her from me?" he hisses, venom dripping from every word.

In the tense standoff, I stand firm, my voice steady. "I'm not here to take anyone from you. I'm here to protect Sophia from you."

He scoffs, his anger fueling his aggression. "You don't know what you've gotten yourself into."

As he takes a menacing step forward, Sophia, trembling but determined, pulls out her phone and dials 911. "I'm calling the police," she says, her fingers shaking as she holds the phone to her ear.

The man's eyes fill with rage and fear. He strikes me hard in the face, and a struggle breaks out as we try to protect ourselves. He is much stronger than me, but I must keep my line to protect Sophia.

Amid the chaos, sirens wail in the distance, growing louder with each passing second.

The sound of approaching police cars sends a shock of adrenaline through us. We continue to fend off the man's relentless attacks, our hearts pounding as we await the arrival of the authorities.

When the police finally arrive, the alley is chaotic and violent. With sirens blaring and lights flashing, officers rush to our aid, pulling the man away and restraining him. Sophia, her voice quivering, tells them about the threats and the danger we faced.

I feel relief as the handcuffs click shut, and they take the man into custody. I'm exhausted.

Sophia removes her scarf, using it to clean the blood from my face. Each touch is gentle, a soothing caress against the aftermath of the confrontation. I wince as she tends to my injuries, her concern evident in her eyes.

"Thank you," I whisper.

Sophia hugs me tightly. It is the first time she hugs me in front of others.

With Sophia's ex behind bars for many years, the darkness that had haunted her past is finally behind us, or, at least, will be left behind for quite a long time. Once hidden behind layers of fear and secrecy, Sophia's sunshine nature shines brightly around me.

One sunny afternoon, we walk in the park. The atmosphere is filled with warmth and hope.

I take Sophia's hand, leading her to a picturesque spot by a tranquil pond. The soft breeze rustles the leaves, and the world pauses as if holding its breath in anticipation.

"Sophia," my voice filled with love and conviction, "from the moment I first saw you, you captured my heart. And now, I want to spend the rest of my life with you." I drop to one knee, producing a small velvet box from my pocket. I open it to reveal a glistening ring that symbolizes my love and commitment. "Sophia," I continue, my eyes locked on to hers, "will you marry me? Will you be mine forever?"

Tears shimmer in her eyes as she smiles, her voice filled with emotion. "Yes, Alex. Yes."

I slip the ring onto her finger, and as our lips meet in a tender and passionate kiss, the world around us fades insignificantly.

In that kiss, we lock in a future together, our hearts beating like a vow of love. The park around us seems to light up, echoing our joy, transforming the world from a place of doubt into our blank canvas. Here, we'll sketch a life rich in love, joy, and a steadfast belief in the power of love to overcome everything.

Holding Sophia's hand, I look into her eyes, pouring my soul without saying a word. "Sophia," my whisper carries every ounce of my love, "our path together is the most beautiful journey. You are everything to me, the truest desire of my heart."

Sophia's eyes glisten with tears, and her smile speaks volumes. My heart overflows as I say, "In your eyes, I've found where I belong. Your laughter brings me happiness, and your love gives my life meaning."

Then, soft and enchanting, Sophia's voice weaves into mine, "Alex, you're my sanctuary, my peace, my endless love. With you, I've discovered a love that breaks all barriers and is endlessly deep and true."

With another kiss, we step into our forever, the world around us disappearing. We stand in the power of our love, an unbreakable bond ready to face whatever comes, together in every dawn and dusk that awaits us.

The Mystery Postcards

I'm Jake, a young mailman in my early twenties. Each morning, I set out on my trusty mail route through the winding streets of our quaint little town. The town itself paints a charming picture with its narrow lanes lined by cozy cottages, their colorful gardens bursting with vibrant blooms.

I enjoy driving on the rolling hills and watching sunlight filter through the canopy of ancient oak trees that seem to arch over the road, casting dappled shadows on the pavement.

I wind my way past the corner bakery, where the scent of freshly baked bread mingles with the morning air. The townsfolk, friendly and familiar, wave as I pass by. Mrs.

Johnson waters her petunias on the porch, and Mr. Adams sits on his porch swing, sipping his coffee.

The town feels like a snapshot of simpler times, where everyone knows each other's name. The only thing that can make a difference to my peaceful daily life is a change in the weather.

Something crucial is absent from my life, and I'm eager to open a new chapter.

One of my old coworkers is retired, and I'm assigned to another side of the town to take over his position. The first morning brings an unexpected twist. I turn a corner onto Elm Street, where an old, abandoned house stands like a forgotten relic of the past. Overgrown vines creep up its weathered facade, and the windows, cloaked in dust, haven't witnessed life in years.

Curiosity piqued, I slow down my mail car, lingering at this forgotten place. Then, something peculiar catches my eye—a stack of unaddressed postcards lies haphazardly in the mailbox by the crumbling gate. These aren't ordinary letters, the words flowing as naturally as the river that meanders through our town. The words on the postcards touch my heart so profoundly; they feel like a warm embrace on a cold winter's day. It's like a wake-up call, making me realize that what I've been missing in my peaceful life is high spirits.

There's a mystique about them, an air of secrecy that pulls me in. Moreover, there's no sender's address on any of them. These postcards seem to have been left here, waiting for someone to stumble upon them to discover their hidden messages.

Without a second thought, I channel my inner Sherlock Holmes and become a detective extraordinaire. I slip on my gloves and yank those mysterious letters out of the mailbox. I hope to return them to the sender.

I need to find the sender. After diligent research through a detective friend, I traced the letters back to an author with a pen named Emily and her PO box. Emily is somewhat of a recluse, rarely seen in public. Her books, though, were celebrated for their lyrical prose and emotional depth.

I return all the postcards to Emily.

One evening, as the sun dips below the horizon and the world is bathed in twilight, I sit down at my tiny desk, a blank sheet of paper before me. Inspired by the words I've found; I decided to reach out to Emily. I do not dare to reveal my identity. I create a pseudonym: "Sam."

I write a letter to Emily. I tell Emily about my discovery of her postcards, how her words have captured my heart, and how I feel a strange connection to the sentiments in her writing. I sign it "Sam the Seeker."

Weeks passed, and I'm still waiting for a response from Emily.

I eagerly check my mailbox each day. Then, one afternoon, nestled among the bills and flyers, I find a letter addressed to "Sam the Seeker." The familiar, elegant script reveals that it's from Emily.

My heart races as I tear open the envelope and read her response.

Her words are every bit as enchanting as those in the un-addressed letters. She thanks me for my letter.

And so, some correspondence begins between us, all while we remain unaware of each other's true identities. Our letters flow back and forth. Emily's letters are like windows into her soul, filled with sensitivity and sharp insights. My letters take on a playful tone, infused with easygoing humor, as I share stories from my daily life. I have never been so open with anyone; our communication knows no limitations as if we are painting the canvas of our hearts with the vibrant colors of our shared experiences.

As our letters continue, a sense of longing and anticipation grows within me. I find myself thinking of Emily more often than not, wondering what she looks like, what her laughter sounds like, and what it would be like to meet the enigmatic author behind the letters that have captured my heart.

***

One quiet evening, I sit at my desk, the soft glow of a desk lamp illuminating the letter before me. The entire message can be summarized in three words: "Can we meet?"

Time suddenly becomes agonizingly slow as I wait for Emily's response with bated breath. One day passes, then a week, and eventually, two weeks.... The weight of my confession and the uncertainty of her reaction hang over me like a storm cloud. I wonder if I've been too forward, too eager to unravel the mystery that has bound us together.

Then, one crisp autumn afternoon, a letter from Emily arrives. She's already in town and provides the meeting location and time.

We meet in a quiet corner of our town, under the canopy of oak trees that line the park by the river. The anticipation of our meeting fills my days with a sense of euphoria. I imagine how she might look, and her voice might sound when I finally face her.

The day of our meeting arrives, and as I stand beneath the familiar oak trees, my heart races with excitement and nervousness. I watch as a figure approaches, which seems to shimmer with the same enchantment that drew me to her letters.

Emily stands before me, her eyes meeting mine with curiosity and warmth. Her smile is as radiant as the sun breaking through the leaves. As we exchange our first words in person, it feels like the natural continuation of a conversation that has been ongoing for months.

"Hey," I say excitedly.

"Hi" is her response, and her voice is soft and calm.

Emily has deep blue eyes that seem to hold the secrets of the ocean depths, and her long, soft hair frames her face with a gentle cascade. Her complexion is pale white, perhaps from spending much of her time indoors, lost in her writing. She wears a simple yet comfortable white top and a long cream skirt. As the wind rustles her clothes and hair, she effortlessly blends with the natural surroundings, a vision of grace and beauty.

As we stroll along the riverbank, our hands brush against each other, igniting a spark of electricity that leaves no doubt in my mind—we are meant to be together.

The sun hangs low on the horizon, casting a warm, golden hue over the tranquil waters of the lake. Emily and I walk in comfortable silence for a while, the soft rustling of leaves and the distant chirping of birds providing the backdrop to our moment.

Eventually, Emily breaks the silence with a thoughtful sigh. "You know," she begins, her voice soft and contemplative, "the owner of that abandoned house I keep sending postcards to was a talented writer I admired since I was young."

I turn to her, curious to hear more.

Her eyes are distant as she recalls memories of the past. "I loved him secretly, but I never dared to tell him my feelings."

Emily turns and looks at me, "He took his own life before I could express my love for him. I am filled with regret. If I had braved enough, perhaps the story could have been rewritten."

My heart aches for her, and I squeeze her hand gently in understanding. "I'm so sorry, Emily," I offer, my voice filled with empathy.

She smiles faintly, her eyes glistening with unshed tears. "Thank you," she says, her voice barely above a whisper. "I miss him so much."

"So, you send him all the postcards?" I inquire.

Emily nods and replies, "Yes. I want him to receive my postcards on his birthday, every holiday, or whenever I miss him."

It dawns on me that all the postcards let her release her emotions. Emily continues to explain, "I hope he can read them in heaven, so I use postcards instead of sealing them into envelopes."

Her story profoundly touches me, and my admiration for her grows with each word she shares.

"Emily," I begin, my voice filled with respect, "your dedication to his memory and beautiful words are truly remarkable."

She looks at me with gratitude shining in her eyes. "Thank you," she says, her voice tinged with emotion. "Since I started talking to you, I feel much better. You understand me well; I thought you should be at least a middle-aged man."

"I'm going to be a middle-aged man, Emily," I assure her. "I respect you and admire your words."

Emily's eyes meet mine, and at that moment, as we continue to walk along the lake, it feels like our souls have intertwined, bound by the shared stories we carry and the unspoken understanding of what it means to love, to grieve, and to find solace in each other's company.

The town that once seemed so ordinary has transformed into a place of magic and wonder, where love has bloomed unexpectedly, like a wildflower in a hidden meadow.

Those postcards, once abandoned and forgotten, have become the thread that weaves our hearts together. We both can feel it through silent gazes.

Emily rents a log cabin near the river in town, where she writes her novel, enjoying the beautiful view of the lake. This allows me to meet her in the following days. She always travels around, staying in beautiful places for a few days before moving on to the next. I think this is her romantic lifestyle.

One sunny afternoon, as I finish my usual rounds, I am drawn to the bustling town square. People mill about, sipping coffee at outdoor cafés and browsing the quaint shops that line the cobbled streets.

And then, as if guided by fate, I see her, Emily.

Emily sits at a small, sunlit table outside a café, her head buried in a book. Her dark hair cascades over her shoulder, and her eyes sparkle with a deep, hidden intensity. She looks like an enchanting stranger, and for a moment, I don't recognize her as my pen pal.

I approach her table and ask if the empty chair across from her is taken. She looks up, her eyes widening in surprise, but she graciously invites me to join her.

As I settle into the chair, I smile. "What are you reading?"

She glances down at the book on the table, her lips curving into a warm smile. "It's a classic, *Pride and Prejudice*. I've always loved the wit and charm of Jane Austen's writing."

I nod, feeling a sense of connection. "I'm a fan of Austen too. Have you read *Sense and Sensibility*?"

Emily's eyes light up. "Yes, I have! It's a beautiful novel. Austen had a unique way of exploring the complexities of human nature and relationships. I hope I can visit her hometown someday."

"Emily, travel can open our minds, allowing us to see the world from different cultures and perspectives."

She responds, "Not always. Travel can also enable me to hide from my world."

Her reply catches me off guard. I wonder why she feels the need to hide from her world.

"Where will you go next?" I ask, attempting to cover my surprise.

"Paris," Emily confesses with a wistful smile. "The city of love and art."

I can't resist the opportunity. "Well, maybe someday, we could go together. Explore the cobblestone streets, sip coffee at sidewalk cafés, and visit the Louvre."

"As my bodyguard?" she asks with a playful tone.

"Lifetime." I lay my hands on her shoulder.

It is the first time I have given my commitment to Emily.

"Thank you, Sam."

Sam! Sam is not my real name.

I must tell Emily the truth. Will our story take an unexpected turn, or will it crumble under the weight of this revelation? I'll see.

"Emily, I'm not Sam, my name is Jake."

"Jake," she hesitantly murmurs, her voice without surprise, "Jack Anderson."

"How do you know my full name?" Her knowledge takes me aback.

"This is a small town; a mailman is a public friend."

"Sorry, Emily, I didn't use my true identity when writing to you. But all my feelings for you are real."

"I know." Emily nods slowly, her gaze steady. "I believe you, Jake."

Relief washes over me, and I smile reassuringly. "I'm glad to hear that."

"It's just... it's been bothering me, and I wanted to discuss it with you." Emily's expression becomes a mixture of skepticism and curiosity. "You like my words, but maybe not who I am."

"What makes you say so?"

"My real name is Alyssa Smith. I'm thirty years old—possibly too old for you. I have a kidney problem, and the doctor said I can only live for another five years unless I replace my kidney."

My heart sinks, shock and sorrow gripping me as I learn of Alyssa's kidney problem and her potentially short time left.

"Alyssa, I will try my best to help you recover. I will share everything with you."

In the days following Alyssa's revelation about her identity and physical condition, I began searching online to find the best doctors who specialize in her condition. I'm determined to do everything to help her.

One chilly evening, we sit in front of her cozy fireplace inside the little cabin, the flickering flames casting dancing shadows across the room. The warmth of the fire mirrors the growing connection between us as we face the challenges ahead.

I turn to Alyssa, my voice filled with sincerity. "Alyssa, I've been researching, and I think you must visit the best-specialized doctor to determine whether your kidney needs to be replaced. We need to make sure you receive the best treatment possible."

"Agreed."

"I can give you all my money, and I can sell my car if you need more."

She looks at me, her eyes reflecting gratitude and vulnerability. "Jake, I appreciate your concern and willingness to support me, but I don't want you to empty your account or sell your car for this. I can take care of myself."

I pause for a moment, touched by her independence and strength. "Alyssa, I want to be there for you in every way possible. It's not about the money; it's about us facing this together. Your health and well-being mean the world to me."

She smiles, her expression softening. "Thank you, Jake. You light the hope in my life. I promise to consider all the options and make the best decisions for my health. I'll no longer ignore it."

As the fire crackles and the room fills with warmth, we hold each other's gaze, knowing that our love has grown stronger through these challenges. I stand up and walk to her. I hug her tightly. We'll face whatever lies ahead.

A week after Thanksgiving snowflakes gently fall from the sky, creating a serene winter wonderland as I continue my mailman's routine. The world around me is blanketed in white, with the snow covering ancient oak trees that seem to arch over the road and the cozy cottages along the way. Residents have already decorated their houses for Christmas, but my thoughts are a thousand miles away, centered on Alyssa.

Alyssa is visiting her doctor today, and unfortunately, I'm bound by my task. I can't be with her during this crucial moment, and it gnaws at me as I navigate the snow-covered streets, delivering letters and parcels.

Then, as I'm on my route, my phone rings. It's from Alyssa. I pull over to the side of the road, my heart pounding in my chest, and answer it.

"Jake," her voice trembling with emotion.

I cannot breathe.

"It's good news. The best gift for Christmas."

I can hardly believe my ears. My grip on the steering wheel tightens, and I struggle to find my voice. "What is it, Alyssa? Please tell me."

She takes a deep breath before speaking, her words carrying a weight that lifts a heavy burden from my shoulders. "I don't need a kidney replacement, Jake. The doctor says my condition is treatable, and I can recover."

Tears well up in my eyes as her words sink in, and I can feel a lump forming in my throat. The weight pressing my chest for weeks suddenly lifts, and relief washes over me.

I lay my head on the steering wheel, overcome with emotion. The snow continues to fall outside, blanketing the world in a peaceful hush. Alyssa's voice on the phone is a lifeline, a beacon of hope, and a promise of a brighter future.

Finally, I find my voice, "Alyssa, I can't express how grateful I am to hear this. It's the best news I could have hoped for."

Alyssa's laughter rings through the phone, a beautiful sound that warms my heart even on a cold winter day. "Jake, we're in this together, and I have hope now. Christmas is going to be a wonderful celebration this year."

I wipe away tears of joy as I sit in the car, overwhelmed by the magnitude of this moment. "You're right, Alyssa," I reply, my voice filled with conviction. "Christmas is going to be the most beautiful celebration, and the best gift of all is having you by my side."

"Jack, I want to invite you to my home. We'll share our first Christmas."

As the snow continues to fall outside, I'm filled with a deep sense of gratitude and love. The world may be covered in white, but at that moment, my heart is bathed in warmth and hope. I accept Alyssa's invitation to spend our first Christmas together at her home in another town.

As I arrive at Alyssa's home, I'm taken aback by its grandeur. It's a huge, expensive house with large windows that stretch from the floor to the twenty-foot ceiling. The rooms are adorned with beautiful Christmas decorations that fill the space with warmth and holiday cheer. It's a sight to behold, and I feel awe and a touch of apprehension.

Alyssa notices my reaction and smiles warmly. "Surprised?" Her eyes twinkle.

I nod, feeling a bit overwhelmed. "I am, Alyssa. Your home is incredible."

She chuckles softly. "I know it might be different from what you're used to, but remember, it's just a house. What matters most is who you're with, not where you are."

I appreciate her reassurance, but I express my uncertainty. "I'm unsure if I can get used to this life, Alyssa. I come from a low-middle-class background, and this is... well, it's a different world."

Alyssa steps closer, her arms wrapping around me in a comforting embrace. She whispers in my ear, her words filled with sincerity, "Jake, remember this—anything that can be accounted for may not be the most valuable thing. The most precious things are often the ones you cannot put a price on. The most valuable thing in my life is you. I was depressed and lonely for a long time, and you have changed my life."

"But, Alyssa, I must be honest about my financial situation. I have only $4,500 in my bank account, and I live in a one-bedroom apartment."

Alyssa responds, "I can share my financial situation too. I make at least $530,000 monthly from my published novels, and I have multiple million dollars in my account."

I've never known anyone personally with such wealth, and for the first time, I feel we may not be a good match. But Alyssa gently reassures me, "Jake, money can't buy happiness. Financial wealth doesn't equate to spiritual richness. Your kindness and beautiful soul are what I need."

Alyssa looks around her grand house and then into my eyes. "For me, living in this house or the log cabin near the lake doesn't make a big difference. This huge house makes me feel isolated at night. Romantic desires don't drive my travels; they're an escape from my small, isolated world."

Her words touch my heart, and I fall deeper in love with her. We smile, and in that moment, my doubts seem to melt away.

As the evening unfolds, we enjoy a romantic dinner by candlelight, savoring each other's company and the delicious food Alyssa has prepared.

After dinner, we cozy by the roaring fireplace, the crackling flames casting a soft, golden glow over the room. Alyssa's hand finds mine, and there, in the warm flickering light, she begins to talk about the letters I sent to her under my fake name, Sam. She shares how she felt when she first read those letters, and her words create an intimate atmosphere that draws us closer.

As the night progresses, our conversation turns quieter and more tender. We gaze into each other's eyes, our feelings laid bare. Then, we share our first night.

"Jake," Emily begins, her voice soft and affectionate, "I can't help but feel like we're living a real-life fairy tale."

"It's just a good start," I reply with confidence. I'll make myself a better man.

Two Builders

In the bright stage lights, I feel like I'm glowing. I stand there, saying lines perfectly, like I've practiced a million times. "I love you," I tell my co-star, sounding so sure. But deep down, I feel lost. Those words aren't mine; they're just lines from a script.

The crowd is like a dark ocean, clapping and cheering. I look out at them, wishing for a real connection, something that's not just acting.

When the show ends and the sound of applause fills the air, I don't feel overwhelmed; I feel lonelier than ever. There's a massive gap between me and the real world, much more than the distance from the stage to the last row of the audience.

I sneak off to my dressing room, away from everyone saying, "Great job."

The door clicks shut, leaving me alone in the quiet. The room is beautiful, but it feels so empty. I stare at my reflection, all dressed up and smiling, but the smile doesn't reach my heart. It's just like the pretend love I show on stage. How can I keep wearing this fake smile in my life, away from the bright lights and applause?

My phone buzzes, a message from a friend: *Drinks tonight?*

I glance at it, then at my reflection. The woman in the mirror looks back, her eyes asking, *For what? Another night of hollow laughter and fleeting glances?*

I change into my regular clothes, leaving behind the famous Emma. The city at night feels less bright; it sounds quieter. I wish for someone who wants to talk to the real me, not the actress. Someone who looks past fame and sees a girl who wants a simple, cozy kind of love.

It's early spring. The city feels alive as I walk, but inside, I feel empty. I will find a man who loves me for who I am, not for my face or fame, who can share the same umbrella with me in the storm.

I call my best friend, Lily; I must meet her at Café Lumière.

I enter the cozy embrace of the café, a world away from the glaring stage lights. Across from me sits Lily, my best friend since our sandbox days, her green eyes reflecting the soft glow of the hanging Edison bulbs.

The café buzzes with life, a soothing contrast to my solitary thoughts.

"You seemed a million miles away on stage tonight," Lily says, concern and curiosity lacing her voice.

I stir my coffee, watching the ripples settle. "Maybe I was," I admit. "Lily, I'm tired of the façade. The applause, the glamour... it's empty."

Lily leans in, her expression earnest. "What you need is someone real. Someone who loves Emma, not the Emma on billboards," she jokes.

I shake my head, a hint of sadness in my tone. "They're drawn to my face, not my soul," I reply. That's the heart of my problem.

"We all have to deal with it. It's like the flu for us," Lily says with a sigh, showing sympathy and weariness. "What do you want to do about it?"

I nod, my mind racing with a budding plan. "What if I try something different, like finding someone online and going on blind dates... but with a twist?" I pause, watching Lily closely for her reaction.

Lily's eyebrows shoot up, a mix of curiosity and confusion in her eyes. "A twist?" she echoes, intrigued but not quite understanding.

"I'll wear makeup, something subtle but noticeable. A birthmark, perhaps, on my forehead."

Lily's eyes widen. "To scare off the shallow ones?"

"Exactly," I say, the plan taking shape. "If someone can look past it, maybe I'll find a real connection."

Lily's laughter fills the space between us, warm and encouraging. "That's brilliant, Emma! It's like your own undercover love mission."

We plot and plan, our conversation a mix of excitement and nerves. I feel a spark, a sense of adventure I haven't felt in years. The waitress refills our cups, her smile an unwitting accomplice to our scheme.

"So, the birthmark," Lily says, her tone severe yet playful. "How big are we talking?"

I touch my forehead, imagining it. "Big enough to be noticed, small enough to be intriguing."

"And if someone sees past it?" she asks.

"Then maybe they can see me," I say, my words a mix of hope and uncertainty.

Our plans laid, we part ways, the night air crisp against my skin.

I park my car inside the garage and walk back home, each step a dance between doubt and determination.

I stand before my mirror that night, tracing an imaginary line on my forehead. For the first time in a long while, I see not just Emma, the actress, but Emma, the dreamer, the hopeful romantic. And with that vision, I drift into sleep, a smile playing on my lips.

Tomorrow, a new act begins.

The next day, I created a profile on an online dating website, using a fake name and an AI photo for a bit of anonymity.

Two weeks pass, and I finally arrange my first blind date—a meeting with Alex, a small business owner. His profile, peppered with photos of him in various entrepreneurial endeavors, boasts a penchant for "deep conversations and meaningful connections." The claim piques my interest, raising the bar for our upcoming encounter.

The clink of fine dinnerware sets the scene as I meet Alex, his eyes momentarily snagging on the birthmark before regaining his composure. "You look... different than I imagined."

I meet his gaze steadily, unfazed. "Appearances can be deceiving," I say with a poised smile.

Disappointment flickers across Alex's face, but I don't let it rattle me. As we order, his cell phone rings. "Excuse me. This is important." He leans back, absorbed in his call, his voice sharp and commanding.

As he launches into a self-aggrandizing monologue about his latest business deal, I listen, my expression composed. "It's all about leveraging your assets," he declares, more to himself than to me.

I interject, aiming to find common ground. "What about outside of work? Any hobbies?"

He barely pauses. "My job is my passion. Why bother with anything else?" His gaze drifts over my shoulder, disinterested.

Curious, I glance back to see a blonde woman laughing with friends. Turning back to Alex, I make my decision. I place money for my meal on the table, my movements deliberate.

"Are you leaving?" Alex finally looks at me, surprised.

"Yes," I reply, my tone calm but firm. "I value my time too much to misspend it." With that, I stand and walk away, my head held high.

The second date is with Darren, an engineer, a seemingly kindhearted soul.

Darren greets me with a smile that somersaults spotting my forehead. "Oh, is that... new?"

"Fresh out of the box," I quip, eager to see where this rabbit hole goes.

"How new? Looks suspiciously like a birthmark." Darren's eyes are glued to my forehead as if it might reveal the universe's secrets.

Over coffee, Darren transforms from Mr. Nice Guy into Captain Fix-It. "You know, laser treatment is almost like magic for birthmarks," he explains, his eyes twinkling with the fervor of a late-night infomercial host.

I try a detour. "So, engineering, huh? Do you build bridges or just cross them?"

He gives a half nod, already rerouting back to the main agenda. "Yeah, bridges, buildings... but let's circle back to your... unique situation. I'm a problem-solver, you see."

"I'm more of a beauty-spot enthusiast," I jest, gesturing to my forehead.

He perks up. "Great to hear! And speaking of beauty, I know a fantastic doctor...."

"No need," I interject. "I'm pretty fond of God's little freebies. This one came without a receipt."

As I escape, feeling more like a fixer-upper than a date, Darren's voice follows me. "Just think about it! I'll text you some top-tier clinics!"

"Thank you," I respond, friendly. Darren is a nice guy, but not my type.

My third date is with Brian, a novel writer in his thirties with striking good looks. He meets me at the bookstore café, his eyes flickering to my forehead with a hint of curiosity.

"Interesting choice for a date," he comments.

"I thought it'd be nice to surround ourselves with stories," I reply, hopeful for a literary connection.

Our conversation initially dances around literature, finding a comfortable rhythm. But as the evening unfolds, Brian's focus wavers, increasingly captured by his phone.

"Sorry," he apologizes without looking up, "just checking the progress of my new book's release."

"That's exciting, congratulations on the publication."

Brian shrugs, a hint of frustration in his tone. "It's okay. Spent fifty bucks on Facebook ads this morning and barely broke even. The world of readers is a mystery," he says, his eyes narrowing in thought.

His nervous energy is palpable.

Seeking lighter territory, I ask, "What's your favorite book?"

Brian offers a distracted nod, his attention stolen by the TV screen behind me. "Oh, lots of them," he murmurs, barely engaging.

I feel disappointed as I realize my competition is a football game. "Maybe we should wrap up for tonight," I suggest gently.

"Sure, sure," he replies, his eyes still glued to the screen. "We should do this again, right?"

I smile, knowing it's just a formality. As I walk away, Brian's gaze remains fixated on the TV.

Outside, the wind plays with my hair, and a wry smile tugs at my lips despite the sting of letdown.

Three blind dates, three unique experiences—it feels like I've just wrapped up an episode of a reality show. It's time to put a full stop to this chapter of my dating life.

I text Lily about my decision.

The following day dawns with a gray overcast, mirroring my mood. I fly back to my hometown; I want to spend a few days with my mom, who understands me the most.

I find solace in the familiar comforts of my childhood home. The aroma of freshly brewed coffee and cinnamon fills the kitchen where my mother, a beacon of warmth and wisdom, moves with a grace that belies her years.

"Rough dates?" she inquires, handing me a steaming mug.

I nod, sinking into a chair. "It's like navigating a minefield of egos and indifference."

She sits across from me, her eyes soft yet piercing. "Emma, you're looking for something real in a world that often isn't. It's brave, but not without its challenges."

I sigh, staring into my coffee. "Maybe I'm chasing a fantasy, Mom. Maybe what I'm looking for doesn't exist."

"Doesn't exist?" She chuckles lightly. "Your father and I found it. It's not a fantasy, Emma. It's just rare."

"But how do you know when to keep going or when to just... stop?" The question hangs in the air, heavy with doubt.

She reaches across the table, her hand covering mine. "You keep going until it feels right to stop. You're strong, Emma. Stronger than you give yourself credit for."

I think of the birthmark, a façade that brought only shallow encounters. "But what if I'm wrong? What if all I find are more disappointments?"

"Then you learn from them." Mom's voice is firm yet kind. "Every disappointment teaches you more about what you truly want. And what you don't."

I ponder her words, a lifeline in a sea of uncertainty. "But it's hard, Mom. It's so hard feeling invisible."

"You're not invisible," she insists. "Not to the people who matter. You're a light, Emma. And the right person will see that. They'll see you, not the actress or birthmark, but you."

Her conviction is a balm to my bruised hope. "What if I never find them?"

She smiles, a blend of nostalgia and confidence. "Then they'll find you. Love has a way of surprising us, often when we least expect it."

I finish my coffee, feeling a renewed sense of purpose. My mother's belief in love for me reignites a spark I thought had dimmed.

I stand up, hugging her tightly. "Thanks, Mom. I needed this."

"Anytime, my dear. And remember, the right person will see your heart, not just your face."

A few days later, I left the warmth of my childhood home and flew back to LA. The sky has cleared, and with it, so has my resolve.

After returning to LA, I settle back into my routine. Life continues as usual until one day, an unexpected opportunity knocks: a notice to audition for a famous movie director. But, as luck would have it, my audition coincides with a brewing storm.

I find myself driving through the storm, anxiety knotting my stomach. Glancing at my watch, I remind myself this meeting is crucial—a potentially career-defining moment. Determined to be punctual, I weave my car through the city's busy streets.

As I make my way, I enter a newly developed city area. It starkly contrasts the familiar urban landscape—a raw, incomplete world of half-built structures, where the earthy smell of wet soil mingles with the scent of construction materials. The storm intensifies, adding a dramatic backdrop to the already daunting journey.

My GPS starts to falter, confused by the new and uncharted roads.

"Not now," I mutter, eyes scanning for any familiar landmark.

Then, disaster strikes—a loud pop, and my car lurches. A nail, hidden amidst construction debris, has punctured my tire. I pull over, the car coming to rest in a muddy field, far from the neat, orderly streets I'm used to.

As I step out, the heavens open up, unleashing a torrent of rain. I wrestle with the jack and spare tire, but the rain is relentless, turning the ground into a treacherous sea of mud. My hands slip on the wet tools, frustration mounting with each failed attempt.

"You look like you could use some help!" a voice calls out through the downpour. I look up, squinting through the rain, to see a man approaching. He's robust, and his solid build indicates his physically demanding job. Despite the storm, there's a kindness in his eyes and a certain rugged handsomeness about him.

"I'm Steven," he says, his voice strong over the roar of the rain, extending a hand already streaked with mud.

"Emma," I reply, attempting a smile that feels more like a grimace. "I'm in a bit of a rush. I have an important meeting and can't afford to be late."

"No worries, Emma. Let's get this sorted quickly." His confidence is infectious.

Steven takes over. His movements are efficient and skilled, even in the pouring rain. The storm has turned my hair into a dripping mess, and my face is streaked with rain and mud, masking any trace of the carefully made-up professional I was this morning.

"Thank you, I... I don't know what I'd do without your help," I say, watching him work, feeling helpless.

He flashes a quick, reassuring smile. "Not a big deal."

I chuckle, the sound muffled by the rain. "It's a big help to me."

The tire is replaced, and Steven doesn't leave me stranded. He walks me back to my car, his boots squelching in the mud. "I'll guide you out of here," he offers. "This place is a labyrinth if you're unfamiliar with it."

We drive slowly, the rain still pouring but less fiercely now. The sun peeks through the clouds, casting a warm, golden light on the sodden earth.

"There, you should be able to make it from here," Steven says, pointing out a familiar road.

"I can't thank you enough, Steven," I say, realizing I don't want this to be the last time I see him.

"Do you... would you mind if I got your contact information?" I ask, fumbling for my phone.

He grins. "Sure thing, Emma. Here, let me type it in for you."

I take one last look in the rearview mirror as I drive away. Steven is still there, watching as he disappears into the fading rain. Despite the chaos of the day and my disheveled appearance, his kindness, and my unexpected resilience leave me feeling surprisingly uplifted.

Pulling up to the meeting venue, I pause for a much-needed respite. I glance at myself in the rearview mirror, taking stock of my appearance. I try to tame my hair with careful movements, now a wild testament to the storm I've just braved. I use a tissue to gently wipe away the mud streaks on my cheeks, inadvertently removing the last traces of my makeup. I take a deep, steadying breath, looking at my reflection—raw, unadorned, yet resolute. "This is me," I think, a quiet resolve building within. "Take it or leave it."

As I enter the audition room, the director, a woman with a stern face and piercing eyes, initially looks taken aback. Her assistant quickly hands me a one-page script. "You have two minutes to prepare," she states crisply.

I scan the script, simultaneously visualizing my performance. Inwardly, I steel myself against the distraction of hundreds of other competitors in the waiting room, pushing aside thoughts of my disheveled appearance.

Standing in the center of the room, I begin. As I delve into the character, I sense the director's demeanor shift. The sharpness in her eyes softens, replaced by what seems like grudging respect.

After my performance, she extended a firm handshake, her initial surprise now morphed into a subtle nod of approval. "Impressive confidence," she comments. "You're the first actress to come to an audition without makeup." The edges of her lips curl into a faint smile, acknowledging my unconventional choice.

Stepping out of the building, a sense of relief washes over me. Successful or not, today's experience is about more than just an audition. I've navigated through a storm and emerged with a newfound inner strength.

My phone vibrates with an incoming message, snapping me back to reality. It's just a few simple words from Steven: *Can you find your way back?* His considerate and timely message brings a warm smile to my face.

Waiting at a red light, I hastily reply: *Of course. Thanks.* My fingers fly over the screen, sending the message into the digital void.

But as the light shifts to green and I start to drive away, a twinge of regret washes over me. In my rush to respond, I realize I've just let slip a perfect chance to see him again.

The city around me buzzes with life, but my mind is still partly back in that muddy field, with the rain pouring down and Steven's steady presence.

As I start the drive home, I expect to meet Steven again.

In the following weeks, I received exhilarating news: I'd been chosen as the lead actress in a movie. Eager to share my gratitude in person, I decide it's time to see Steven again.

Sitting in my quiet living room, the box of chocolates beside me, I hesitate momentarily before picking up my phone. My fingers hover over Steven's contact, the one he entered in the storm. I tap the call button.

"Hey, Steven, it's Emma," I say when he answers, my voice steadier than I feel. "I wanted to properly thank you for your help. Could we meet at that coffee shop near the construction site where you're working?"

There's a brief pause, and his warm voice fills my ear. "Sure, Emma, that sounds great. When were you thinking?"

"How about this afternoon, roughly after thirty minutes?" I suggest, hoping it's not too soon.

"That works for me. See you then, Emma."

As I end the call, I'm on my way.

I push open the door to the coffee shop, a box of chocolates tucked under my arm. The bell above the door chimes as I scan the room. I spot him near the window, his robust frame hunched over a small table, engrossed in his phone.

"Hey, Steven," I call out as I approach. He looks up, and his face breaks into a smile, his eyes lighting up in recognition.

"Emma, right? The damsel in distress from the construction field?" he teases, standing to greet me.

I laugh, setting the box on the table. "Guilty as charged. I brought these as a thank-you. You were a lifesaver."

He accepts the box. "Wow, this is too much, but thank you." His tone is genuine. He gestures for me to sit down.

As we settle into our seats, I order a coffee, and he gets a black tea.

"So, how did the meeting go after all that?" he asks, leaning forward, genuinely interested.

"It went well. I arrived right on time," I reply, chuckling at the memory.

I find myself studying him, the lines of his face, the way his eyes crinkle when he laughs. He's ruggedly handsome, and the kindness about him is endearing. But there's something I need to know.

"So, Steven, you are the builder, "I begin, a little hesitant. "Is there a Mrs. Builder in your life?"

"No."

"Maybe a girlfriend?"

"No."

"Why?" I keep digging.

He looks surprised momentarily, then laughs, a deep, hearty sound. "No, no Mrs. Builder. And no girlfriend either. My work keeps me pretty busy."

I feel a flutter of relief mixed with excitement. "I can imagine. It must be fulfilling, creating something lasting."

"Yeah, it is," he agrees, his eyes meeting mine. "What about you? Anyone waiting for you to come home?"

"No, just me," I reply, feeling a warmth spread through me at the thought that maybe, just maybe, there's a possibility here.

"Unbelievable," Steven says with a smile, his eyes twinkling with humor and admiration. "A girl like you... must have admirers lining up."

I meet his gaze, a playful yet determined glint in my own. "I prefer to be the one making the selections," I reply, my tone lighthearted but confident.

"What do you make for a living?"

"I'm a manager of a Walmart."

As we part ways, Steven hesitates for a moment. "Would you... maybe want to grab dinner sometime?" he asks, a hopeful note in his voice.

I smile, feeling a rush of happiness. "I'd like that." I am already looking forward to seeing him again.

Stepping out of the coffee shop, I know this is the beginning of something promising with Steven.

A month later, as autumn paints the city in hues of amber and rust, our relationship blossoms with a newfound lightness.

On a brisk evening, Steven invites me to his cozy apartment with a view of the city skyline. He cooks dinner, each dish a testament to his attention to detail and care. We dine to the backdrop of soft jazz, the city lights twinkling like distant stars.

After dinner, he pulls out an old photo album. It's a window into his past, each picture a story. He points to a young boy with a makeshift hard hat. "I, age seven, 'supervising' my dad's garage project."

I laugh, touched by the glimpse into his childhood.

Then he grows quiet, turning to a photo of a younger him with a woman, their arms wrapped around each other. "That's Sara," he says, his voice a whisper. "We were engaged."

The air shifts, heavy with unspoken words. "What happened?" I ask gently.

He closes the album, his eyes meeting mine. "She passed away in a car accident just months before the wedding."

The pain in his voice is palpable, a wound still fresh despite the years. "I'm so sorry, Steven," I say, my heart aching for his loss.

He nods thoughtfully. "We all have scars. The differences lie in their size and depth."

I gently take his hand, feeling a connection deeper than words. "And in how we choose to heal them," I add softly, meeting his gaze.

That night, as I lie in his arms, enveloped in the comforting rhythm of his heartbeat, a profound realization washes over me. In the whispers of the night, it becomes clear just how deeply we've come to love each other.

Autumn's embrace turns to winter's chill, and with it comes an evening that feels ripe with unspoken words. Steven and I sit in his living room, a fire crackling in the hearth, casting a warm glow over us.

I've just returned from my movie shoot, and the experience is still vivid. Before leaving, I told Steven I needed to go away for months of training. But the truth is, it was a lie.

As the weight of my dishonesty settles in, I'm overwhelmed with guilt.

The need to make things right, to confess and apologize, presses urgently against my conscience. I know I can't let this lie stand between us—it's not the foundation I want for whatever might bloom between Steven and me.

Steven looks at me, a question in his eyes. "You've been quiet tonight. What's on your mind, Emma?"

I draw a deep breath, the weight of my secret pressing against my chest. "Steven, there's something I need to tell you. Something about me that I've kept hidden."

He leans forward, his expression open, encouraging. "You can tell me anything, Emma."

I pause, gathering the courage. "It's about my life... my career. I'm not just Emma. I'm Emma Delaney, the actress."

The words hang in the air, a fragile confession. Steven's expression shifts, a mixture of surprise and confusion.

"The Emma Delaney?" he asks, disbelief coloring his tone.

I nod, my heart racing. "Yes. I kept it hidden because I wanted someone to see me, the real me, not the actress or the celebrity."

Steven sits back, processing the revelation, his silence like a widening gulf between us.

"Emma, why didn't you tell me sooner?" His voice is soft but holds an undercurrent of hurt.

"I was scared," I whisper. "Scared that you'd see me differently, that our connection would change."

He looks into the fire, contemplation etched on his face. "I understand why you did it, but it feels like you didn't trust me."

The truth of his words stings. "I do trust you, Steven. More than anyone. It's just that... this world I'm in, finding something real is hard. What we have it's the most genuine thing I've experienced."

He turns to me, his eyes searching mine. "Emma, I've fallen for you, for the woman I've come to know. Your world and fame don't change how I feel."

Relief washes over me, a wave of gratitude and love. "I'm so sorry, Steven. I never wanted to hurt you."

He takes my hand, his grip firm yet gentle. "I get it, Emma. And I'm not going anywhere. But let's promise each other no more secrets."

I nod, a promise sealed in our entwined hands. "No more secrets," I echo.

We sit quietly, warmed by the fire. It's like the steady flame inside us. Telling Steven the truth has opened my heart, and his understanding shows me a love that's more than just being famous or rich.

Outside, the winter wind keeps blowing, but inside, we feel peaceful. Here, by the fire, it's just Steven and me, our hearts together, sharing a solid love because we're honest and trust each other.

Spring is here. Steven and I relax in his small, cozy garden on a sunny Sunday afternoon. It feels like we're a world away from the busy life I'm used to. Here, in this simple moment, we find our little paradise.

We sit on an old bench, holding hands and watching the sunlight play through the leaves. The gentle breeze brings the smell of flowers, filling the air with calmness and new beginnings.

"I always dreamed of this," I say softly, resting my head on his shoulder. "Finding peace in simple things."

Steven laughs, a deep sound that's comforting. "Life's strange like that. The best parts are often hidden in the simplest moments."

I look up at him, my heart full. "With you, Steven, every moment is special."

He kisses my forehead softly. "You've taught me that love is found not in big gestures but in these quiet times together."

The engagement ring on my finger sparkles in the sunlight, a symbol of our love.

Printed in Great Britain
by Amazon

40101754R00057